D1406546

Twinkle

Illustrated by Scott M. Fischer

SIMON & SCHUSTER BOOKS FOR YOUNG READERS • An imprint of Simon & Schuster Children's Publishing Division
1230 Avenue of the Americas, New York, New York 10020 • Illustrations copyright © 2007 by Scott Fischer • All rights reserved, including the
right of reproduction in whole or in part in any form. • SIMON & SCHUSTER BOOKS FOR YOUNG READERS is a trademark of Simon & Schuster, Inc. •
Book design by Daniel Roode • The text for this book is set in Plumbsky. • The illustrations for this book are rendered in Photoshop and graphite.
• Manufactured in Malaysia • 10 9 8 7 6 5 4 3 2 1 • CIP data for this book is available from the Library of Congress. •
ISBN-13: 978-1-4169-3980-1 • ISBN-10: 1-4169-3980-6

Twinkle

Illustrated by Scott M. Fischer

Simon & Schuster Books for Young Readers

New York   London   Toronto   Sydney

Twinkle, twinkle, little star,
How I wonder what you are!

Up above the world so high,
Like a diamond in the sky.

When the blazing sun is gone,
When he nothing shines upon,
Then you show your little light,
Twinkle, twinkle, all the night.

Then the traveller in the dark
Thanks you for your tiny spark;

He could not see which way to go
If you did not twinkle so.

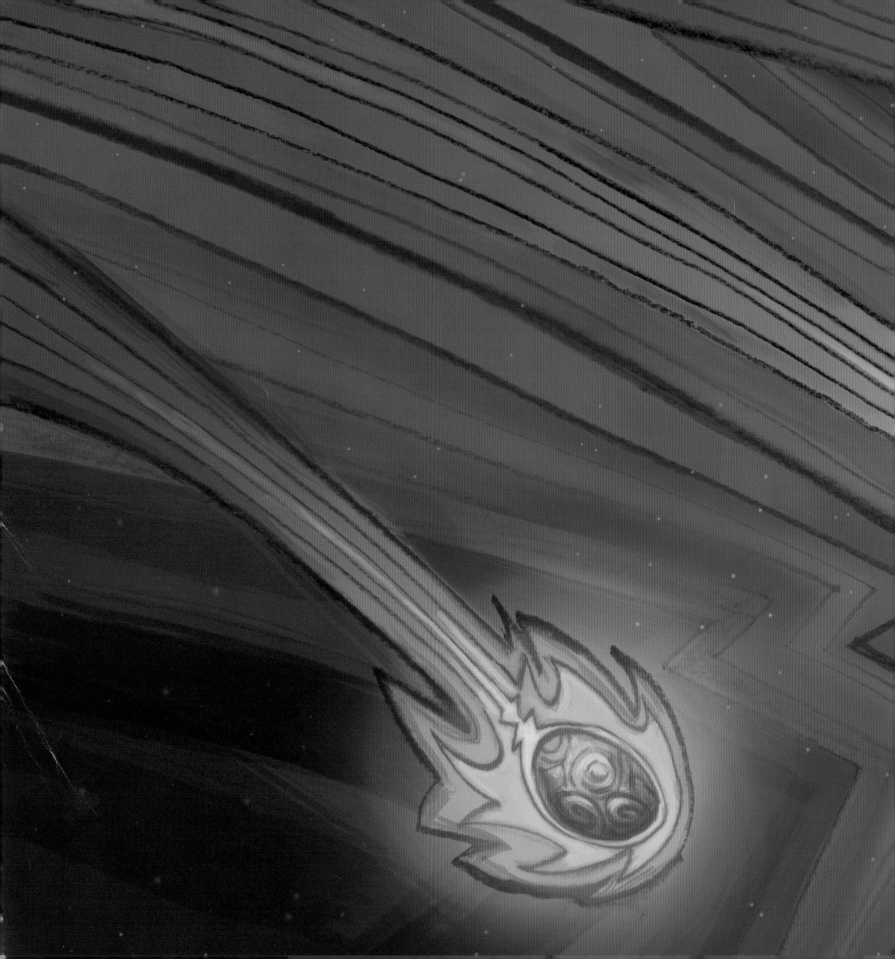

In the dark blue sky you keep,
And often through my curtains peep,

For you never shut your eye
Till the sun is in the sky,

As your bright and tiny spark
Lights the traveller in the dark:

For you never shut your eye
Till the sun is in the sky.

In the dark blue sky you keep,
And often through my curtains peep,

He could not see which way to go
If you did not twinkle so.

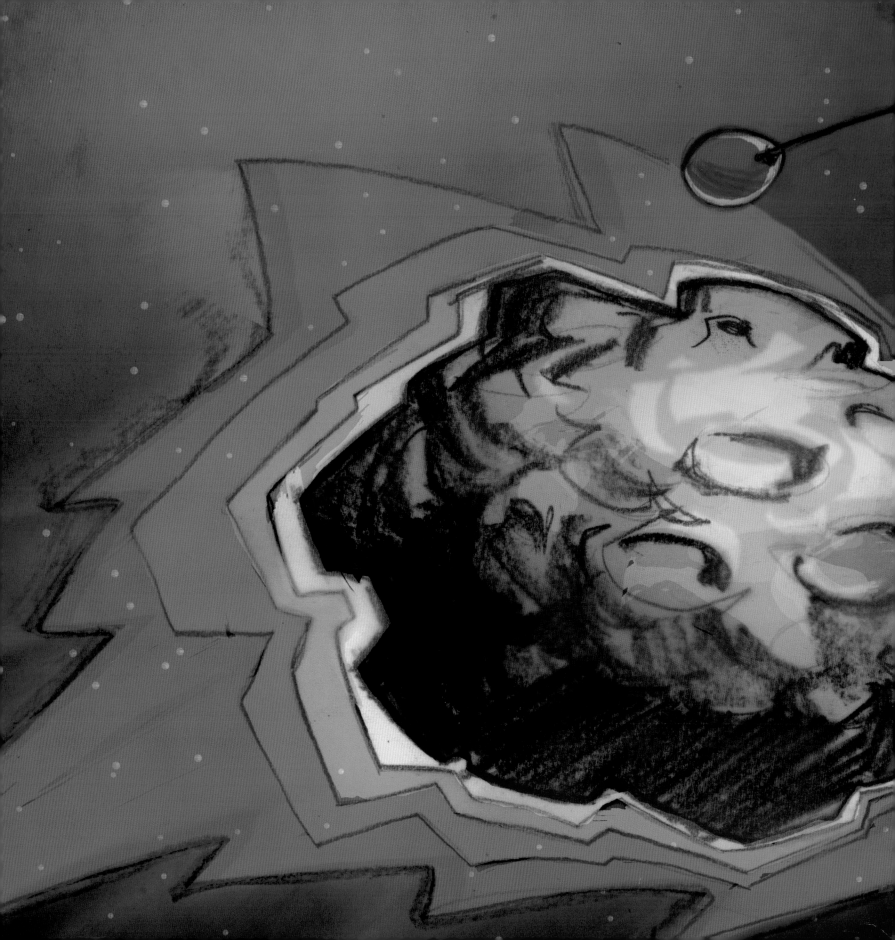

Then the traveller in the dark
Thanks you for your tiny spark;

Twinkle, twinkle, all the night.

When the blazing sun is gone,
When he nothing shines upon,
Then you show your little light,

Up above the world so high,
Like a diamond in the sky.

Twinkle, twinkle, little star,